UP ON THE
MOUNTAIN

Peter Donnelly

GILL BOOKS

Up on the mountain we followed
a small path through the woods.

Up on the mountain we collected
beautiful leaves of every colour.

Up on the mountain we heard songbirds whistle their tunes.

Up on the mountain we
threw acorns at Daddy.

Up on the mountain Sammy
chased a squirrel up a tree.

Up on the mountain we
picked bluebells together.

Up on the mountain we sheltered
beneath a giant oak tree.

Up on the mountain we saw
our little yellow house below.

Up on the mountain the sun
warmed our smiles.

Up on the mountain we saw a great big ocean in the distance.

Up on the mountain we could almost touch the clouds.

Up on the mountain an eagle soared high above us.

Up on the mountain the air
was clear and fresh.

Up on the mountain
WE FELT ALIVE!

Now we are sleepyheads.
But tomorrow, can we please
go up on the mountain again?